MALANAD MYSTERIES

2

BASED ON REAL LIFE STORIES

HARIHAR PAI

Disclaimer:

While the stories are based on real life events, the characters and their conversation are fictionalised. Linking them to any person either living or dead is purely coincidental.

DEDICATED TO THE PEOPLE OF

MALNAD.

PREFACE

The Malnad region stands as a testament to nature's splendour, a place of awe-inspiring beauty that truly demands first-hand experience to be fully grasped. Its breath-taking landscapes are complemented by the genuine warmth and hospitality of its people, rendering it a truly remarkable destination. Each town within this region harbours its own fascinating stories waiting to be discovered.

Following the positive reception of Malnad Mysteries , I was inspired to delve deeper into the tales of Malnad for Malnad Mysteries 2. Though individuals may come and go, their stories endure. Recognizing the value of preserving these captivating narratives for future generations, I chose to immortalize them in writing. These stories offer a glimpse into the lives of remarkable individuals and their unique perspectives on the world around them. To safeguard their privacy, I have altered the names of certain individuals. The stories are rooted in true events, but certain conversations have been fictionalized to vividly depict scenarios, enabling readers to immerse themselves in the narrative and imagine the unfolding scenes with realism.

While some of these stories remain shrouded in secrecy, it's possible that you may have heard them passed down through your own family's history. If you possess any additional information about these tales, I invite you to reach out to me at MalnadMysteries@gmail.com. Together, let us unveil the mysteries of Malnad.

ACKNOWLEDGEMENTS

This book owes its existence to the exceptional storytellers who possess the remarkable talent of transporting us to imaginative realms. These often unrecognised heroes come from diverse backgrounds, spanning from small towns to bustling cities, and each one carries a unique tale to share. Without their contributions, this book would not have come to fruition.

I want to express my sincere gratitude to all the readers who will contribute to ensuring that these stories are passed down to future generations. Your support holds immense significance to me.

Furthermore, I extend my heartfelt appreciation to my parents, Mr. Nagesh Pai and Mrs. Vinita Pai, who accompanied me on countless journeys and shared their captivating narratives.

I must also convey my special thanks to my mentors, Nagendra Reddy and Babu Prasad, for their invaluable guidance and support.

Additionally, I would like to express my gratitude to the Pai and Mahale families for their consistent encouragement throughout this writing journey.

A special shoutout goes to Rudragouda Sanakal for his role as a beta reader, providing valuable insights that significantly improved the quality of the book.

I want to give a big shoutout to Rakesh Halijol and Nilay Shekhar for creating the trailer video to promote the book. Their efforts truly brought the essence of the book to life in an engaging and captivating way.

TABLE OF CONTENTS

1. IT FOLLOWS YOU

Despite the compulsion to attend his cousin's wedding and the added pressure of being showcased as a potential future groom, Rahul couldn't deny the allure of the Western Ghats.

As he continued his drive, he found himself captivated by the enchanting landscapes and the sense of adventure that accompanied the journey. The dense forests that lined the roads were a sanctuary for a diverse range of wildlife. Rahul caught glimpses of exotic birds perched on tree branches, their vibrant plumage adding splashes of colour to the verdant surroundings. The occasional glimpse of shy animals disappearing into the foliage reminded Rahul of the delicate balance between human existence and the natural world.

The weather in the Western Ghats was notorious for its unpredictability. Sudden showers and mist obscured the views, adding an element of mystique to the journey. While it presented a challenge for driving, it also lent an ethereal beauty to the surroundings.

As Rahul continued driving through the Western Ghats, the thought of taking a rest and finding a place to relieve himself crossed his mind. The long and challenging drive had made him aware of his physical needs, and finding a suitable spot to rest became a priority.

Aware of the limited amenities in the remote areas of the Western Ghats, Rahul kept an eye out for any signs of rest areas, public facilities, or even a suitable spot by the roadside. However, the dense forests and winding roads made it difficult to come across such conveniences.

After driving for some time, Rahul finally spotted a small clearing by the roadside that seemed relatively secluded. Assessing the surroundings to ensure his safety, he decided to pull over and take a short break. He parked his vehicle in a suitable spot and stepped out, grateful for the chance to stretch his legs and attend to his personal needs.

As Rahul took a moment to relieve himself in the serene clearing, a sudden cold breeze swept through the area, enveloping him in its embrace. The unexpected chill sent a shiver down his spine, causing him to pause and become acutely aware of his surroundings. Accompanying the cold breeze was a delicate fragrance that filled the air, permeating his senses. The sweet scent of jasmine wafted through the clearing, infusing the atmosphere with its enchanting aroma. The fragrance seemed to blend harmoniously with the natural surroundings, adding an ethereal quality to the moment.

Amidst the gentle touch of the breeze and the captivating fragrance of jasmine, Rahul thought he heard a faint whisper carried by the wind. The whisper, barely audible, seemed to carry a message or a hint of something beyond his comprehension. Feeling a mix of intrigue and trepidation, Rahul couldn't shake off the thought of the whispered voice belonging to a woman. The notion seemed improbable and even hallucinatory, given the remote location of the forest. His mind raced with questions and concerns, unsure of what to make of the experience.

Fuelled by a sense of unease, Rahul swiftly made his way back to his car. The engine roared to life, and he accelerated, leaving the clearing and the mysterious encounter behind. Fear and rationality took precedence over curiosity, prompting him to distance himself from the unfamiliar and potentially unsettling situation.

As the car sped through the winding roads of the Western Ghats, Rahul couldn't help but glance back at the clearing, half-expecting to see a glimpse of the woman whom he thought he had heard. However, the forest remained tranquil and undisturbed, offering no indication of any supernatural presence.

With each passing mile, Rahul attempted to dismiss the incident as a figment of his imagination, a trick played by his mind amidst the unfamiliar surroundings. He focused on the task at hand—driving safely and reaching his destination.

****

As Rahul reached home, he was warmly greeted by his mother, who had prepared his favourite dish, Payasam, in anticipation of his arrival.

In the midst of his family's joyful reunion, Rahul shared tales and caught up on the events of the past eight months, during which he had been away from home. Laughter and heartfelt conversations filled the room, creating a sense of warmth and togetherness. As the night progressed and the topics of conversation dwindled, Rahul eventually retired to his bed.

However, tonight felt different for him. He couldn't shake the sensation of a lingering scent of jasmine in the air, reminiscent of the fragrance that had enchanted him in the Western Ghats. Its inexplicable presence seemed to follow him, defying logical explanation.

Rahul pondered, "This fragrance is starting to grate on my nerves. Could this be phantosmia, an olfactory hallucination?" With a sigh, he pulled the blanket over his head, letting the weariness of the day lull him into sleep.

In the early hours of the morning, Rahul found himself enveloped in a strange dream. A gentle breeze swept through his bedroom, causing the woman's hair to flutter around her. The breeze whisked away the jasmine braid adorning her hair, and delicate flowers tumbled down, landing upon him. With a sudden start, Rahul awoke from the dream, jolted by its vividness, only to realize it had been nothing more than a figment of his imagination.

(Artistic Impression Lady in Jasmine)

****

In the days following the intense dream and lingering scent of jasmine, Rahul found himself unable to shake off the fragrance that seemed to follow him. The aroma of jasmine permeated his senses, persisting even in the most mundane of settings.

As Rahul attended the wedding festivities, the scent of jasmine seemed to surround him, evoking memories of his dream and the enigmatic encounter. The fragrance became intertwined with the atmosphere of the marriage hall, filling the air with its alluring presence.

Curious about the lingering fragrance of jasmine, Rahul approached a couple of girls at the wedding venue and inquired about it. Unaware of his genuine interest and mistaking his question as an attempt to flirt, they dismissed his inquiry with playful smiles and teasing remarks, considering him to be a flirtatious individual. Rahul, taken aback by their response, felt a mix of embarrassment and frustration, realising that his innocent curiosity had been misinterpreted.

The once-vibrant Rahul had become introspective, spending hours immersed in deep thought and reflection. Nightmares plagued his sleep, with the persistent whispers and overwhelming scent of jasmine growing more pronounced in his subconscious.

****

One fateful night, as Rahul slept, he felt the sensation of soft hands shaking him, as if someone were trying to wake him. He awoke with a jolt, half-seeing a blurry figure of a woman in white with an indistinct smile. Yet, upon fully waking, Rahul found himself alone once more. The realization that it was merely a dream brought him a fleeting sense of relief, but sleep eluded him for the rest of the night.

Seeking solace, Rahul retreated to the washroom, splashing water on his face in an attempt to shake off the unsettling experience. With towel in hand, he turned towards the mirror to dry himself, only to be met with a chilling sight. A woman draped in a saree, jasmine adorning her hair, stood behind him, her gentle smile sending shivers down his spine.

Confusion clouded his thoughts as he grappled with the possibility that he might still be trapped within the confines of his dream, or if this encounter transcended the boundaries of his imagination. Too frightened to confront the apparition, Rahul cried out for his mother, his voice echoing through the empty room.

As his parents hurried to his side, Rahul turned to the mirror once more, only to find the figure had vanished.

****

Rahul: Mom, I'm really freaked out by something that happened to me. I need your help.

Mother: Oh, sweetheart, of course. Sit down and tell me all about it. I'm here for you.

Rahul: Okay, so I was driving through the Western Ghats, and I decided to stop at this clearing for a break. Suddenly, I smelled jasmine out of nowhere, and it felt like I could hear a woman whispering. It was so vivid, Mom.

Mother: That sounds intense, Rahul. Are you sure it wasn't just your mind playing tricks on you?

Rahul: I wish it was, but even after I got home, the smell of jasmine stuck around. And today, I swear I saw that woman in the mirror.

Mother: We can't ignore this. Maybe we should talk to Swamiji. He might have some insights into what's happening.

Rahul: Yeah, let's do that. I hope he can help me figure this out.

****

The he next day, Rahul and his mother made their way to Swamiji's abode.

Swamiji welcomed them warmly, his serene presence comforting Rahul's anxious heart.

"Please, my child," Swamiji said with a gentle smile, "share with me what troubles your mind."

Rahul recounted his unsettling experiences in the Western Ghats, the lingering scent of jasmine, and the mysterious appearance of the woman in the mirror.

Swamiji listened attentively before speaking, "Rahul, during your journey, were there any naughty thoughts or emotions that occupied your mind?"

Rahul hesitated for a moment, then replied, "Well, Swamiji, my mother is present here..."

Understanding Rahul's embarrassment, Swamiji reassured him, "There is no shame, my child. Our thoughts are natural, but they can sometimes attract energies beyond our understanding."

Rahul, relieved by Swamiji's understanding, asked, "What can I do to make it stop?"

"We shall perform a cleansing ritual," Swamiji explained. "Together, we will create a sacred space and guide the spirit towards tranquillity."

Rahul: Thank you, Swamiji. I'll do whatever it takes to put an end to this.

Swamiji performs a cleansing ritual using sacred herbs, incense, camphor, and chants to create a sacred space for the ritual. Rahul follows Swamiji's instructions and participates with utmost faith.

Swamiji: Now, Rahul, visualise the presence of the woman and the fragrance of jasmine. In your mind, express your compassion and tell her it's time to release any attachment and move towards the divine realm.

Rahul: (closing his eyes, speaking with conviction) Spirit, I understand your presence, but it's time to find peace and let go of any earthly attachments. I release you with love and compassion. Move towards the divine light and find eternal serenity. Rahul took deep breaths, allowing the scent of camphor to envelop him. As Rahul repeats his words, a peaceful energy fills the room, and the fragrance of jasmine slowly dissipates.

Rahul: Thank you so much, Swamiji. I feel much better now. Swamiji, I don't believe in supernatural occurrences. Could it have just been my mind playing tricks on me?

Swamiji: Whatever it may have been, it's resolved now. Let go of any doubts and focus on peace. And perhaps be mindful of your naughty thoughts when you're alone next time. *He chuckles.*

2. MESSAGE ON THE WALL

Place Of Origin : Karwar, Karnataka.

Lakshmi Bai sat on the porch of her lone tiled house, a weary smile playing on her lips as she watched her nephew, Ajay, frolic in the yard.

"Careful, Ajay! Don't run too fast," Lakshmi Bai called out, her voice filled with love and concern. Ajay laughed and twirled around, his small face glowing with happiness.

"Aunty, look at me! I'm flying like a bird!" Lakshmi Bai chuckled, her heart filled with joy at the sight of Ajay's innocent delight.

He was the only ray of sunshine in her life, a source of joy amidst the darkness that surrounded her. Her husband's alcoholism had extinguished the spark in her eyes, leaving her disinterested and disheartened.

The brief two-month leave her husband took from the army each year brought a mix of emotions. While his return meant moments of companionship, it also meant enduring the storm of his alcoholic tantrums that shattered the tranquilly of their home. The remaining ten months of the year, when he was away, offered temporary relief from the chaos, providing a respite from his addiction.

The memory of her daughter's marriage remained a source of solace for Lakshmi Bai. It was the one true happiness she had experienced—seeing her daughter find love and security within a good family. The thought of her daughter's well-being brought a warm glow to her heart, reminding her that there were brighter moments in life to hold onto.

Their lone tiled house stood amidst a vast, dry farm. Majestic mango trees created a natural barrier, obscuring the views beyond. Frequent power cuts added to her struggles, leaving her in darkness for hours on end. Apart from gazing at the road that meandered through the farm, there was little else to distract Lakshmi Bai from the monotony and hardships of her life.

However, when Ajay came to visit, a newfound energy filled their humble abode. Their time together was filled with laughter and play, creating pockets of joy within the confines of their home. Lakshmi Bai devoted herself to showering Ajay with love and attention, cherishing every moment they shared.

****

As Lakshmi Bai was engrossed in playing with Ajay at the entrance of the house, her attention fully captured by their joyful interaction, she failed to notice the beggar slipping into the compound. It was only when the beggar's voice, tinged with an unnerving tone, pierced through the air that Lakshmi Bai's senses jolted back to reality.

Startled, Lakshmi Bai turned her gaze towards the source of the strange voice and found the beggar standing a mere 10 feet away. She couldn't help but feel a wave of unease wash over her. The beggar's enigmatic smile only deepened her sense of foreboding.

In the stifling heat of the Karwar afternoon, time seemed to stand still as Lakshmi Bai grappled with the strange presence before her.

The beggar's appearance was unsettling, his ragged clothes clinging to his gaunt frame, his face weathered by a life of hardship. His outstretched begging bowl spoke volumes about his struggles.

But it was his voice that sent a chill down Lakshmi Bai's spine. Each word he spoke seemed to carry a hidden meaning, a mysterious tone that held her captive. His request for a meal sounded like more than just hunger—it was as if he knew something she didn't.

Once more, the beggar's plea pierced the air, echoing with a haunting insistence, "Can I have some meals?"

Despite her growing unease, a wave of compassion washed over her, momentarily overpowering her confusion.

As if in a trance, Lakshmi Bai found herself drawn to the kitchen, her mind clouded by the strange encounter. With mechanical movements, she began assembling food onto a plate, her actions detached from her usual awareness.

The cry of Ajay shattered the fog of fear clouding Lakshmi Bai's mind, jolting her back to reality with a surge of panic. She realised, with horror, that she had left Ajay alone outside with the mysterious beggar.

In a frantic instant, Lakshmi Bai's subconscious shattered, and she turned around, her heart pounding in her chest. To her horror, the beggar stood ominously close behind her, his eerie smile etched into her memory like a haunting image. His yellowed teeth seemed to gleam in the dim light, and the unsettling curve of his lips sent shivers down her spine.

Trapped in the confined space of the kitchen, Lakshmi Bai felt suffocated by its limited exits. A cry for help caught in her throat, but fear rendered her voice useless. Paralysed, she stood there, unable to move or make a sound, as the beggar's gaze bore into her with an intensity that froze her in place. Then, in a blink, he vanished into thin air, leaving Lakshmi Bai bewildered and trembling.

Confused and terrified, she rushed outside to find Ajay, her heart pounding with relief as she saw him still playing innocently.

Lakshmi Bai's mind swirled in disarray, grappling with the unsettling events that had just unfolded. Was it all a trick of her imagination, or something more sinister? Despite her attempts to dismiss it, she couldn't shake the feeling that she had narrowly escaped a looming threat.

As she stood there, her gaze scanning the empty road before her, confusion clouded her thoughts. There was no trace of the beggar, no sign of his presence, leaving her to question her own perception of reality. Had she hallucinated in the solitude of the kitchen? And if so, where had the beggar vanished to?

Seeking solace in the comforting embrace of Ajay, Lakshmi Bai hugged him tightly, her heart yearning for reassurance. She tried to convince herself that the encounter with the beggar was nothing more than a trick of her mind, a product of the stress and unease that had plagued her life.

Yet, as she led Ajay back into the kitchen, her eyes fell upon a chilling sight. There, imprinted on the wall before her, were five distinct finger marks, as if burned into the surface. The eerie remnants of an adult's touch sent a shiver down her spine, dispelling any notion that the encounter had been a mere hallucination.

(Artistic Impression Mark On The Wall)

There was something more at play, something beyond her understanding.

With Ajay still by her side, she took a step back, her mind racing to comprehend the significance of those mysterious marks. What had transpired in this very kitchen? Who—or what—had left behind such an indelible and unsettling trace? Lakshmi Bai's heart raced; her mind was flooded with a mix of fear and confusion.

As time passed, Lakshmi Bai found herself unable to shake off the memory of that mysterious encounter. The true nature of the beggar and the significance of the lingering handprint on the wall continued to elude her, casting a shadow over her daily life.

Though the initial fear and uncertainty had gradually faded, the handprint remained as a silent testament to the inexplicable events of that day. Life had moved forward, but the mystery persisted, a constant reminder of the unknown forces that lurked in the corners of her world.

****

Years later, Ajay, now a grown man, found himself reminiscing about that fateful day with his college friend, Hari. As they sat in their dorm room at GAS College in Karwar, Ajay decided to share the spine-chilling story of the beggar and the mysterious handprint that had plagued his childhood.

Hari listened intently as Ajay recounted the details—the strange smile, the disappearing beggar, and the chilling handprint on the kitchen wall. He couldn't help but feel captivated by the eerie tale unfolding before him. The two friends wondered about the true nature of the beggar and the meaning behind that handprint. Had it been a malevolent spirit that had briefly crossed paths with Lakshmi Bai, leaving its mark as a lingering reminder of its presence?

Then, in 2015, a decade after Lakshmi Bai had passed away, her relatives made the decision to renovate the old house. The walls were whitewashed, symbolising a fresh start for the dwelling that had borne witness to so much.

And so, the mark on the wall, the final vestige of that mysterious encounter, was erased from existence. It was as if the house was bidding farewell to the unsettling chapter that had played out within its walls, ready to welcome a new era of tranquilly and peace.

Though the handprint was no longer visible, the story of the beggar and the enigmatic mark on the wall would continue to be shared and remembered by those who knew the tale. It would fade into the realm of folklore, whispered by future generations, forever weaving a tapestry of curiosity and intrigue around the lone tiled house in the middle of the dry farm, where the mango trees once obstructed the views and where the handprint had left its ghostly impression for nearly three decades.

3. UNWANTED LUCK

The marriage hall plunged into an eerie silence, with all eyes fixed on the enigmatic woman who had just made her entrance. Whispers swirled through the air, creating a palpable sense of anticipation.

As the woman gracefully manoeuvred through the sea of people, she felt a mix of discomfort and intrigue. Clutching the border of her saree, she made her way towards the stage where the newlyweds stood. Surprisingly, it was the woman, Shalini, who was capturing more attention than the radiant bride.

A subtle smile graced her face, revealing a mix of determination and acceptance that the multitude of eyes held little significance to her. Shalini, a simple village woman, found herself at the epicentre of a storm of comparisons to the legendary Shivaji Maharaja, all due to a single incident.

****

As I collected the initial details from others after the wedding feast, I approached her. A faint smile hinted at her weariness, but she graciously shared the detailed account, destined to become a tale for the ages.

Shalini's story unfolded as she recounted the events of that fateful summer night in 1998. "It was a Friday," she began, her voice carrying the weight of memory. "My aunt and I were at home when, around 11:00 pm, our dog Rocky, a large German Shepherd, started barking. At first, we thought nothing of it, assuming he had spotted some small creature in the darkness."

She paused, the atmosphere around us seeming to shift as she continued. "But Rocky's bark soon took on an unsettling tone. The night fell silent, thick with tension. Worried for our furry companion, we went to look for him, only to find his usual spot empty."

Shalini's grip tightened on her saree as she spoke, reliving the fear of that moment. "Armed with nothing but a stick and a torch, I ventured into the shadows of the nearby cashew plantations, calling out Rocky's name into the darkness. It felt as though the very night itself held its breath, waiting for some unseen danger to reveal itself."

Her eyes glazed over momentarily as she recalled the sensation. "And then, about 100 metres into the plantations, I felt it—a subtle movement in the stillness. It sent a shiver down my spine, a warning of something lurking just beyond the reach of my torchlight."

Shalini's words hung heavy in the air as she shared the intensity of her experience. "Do you ever know how it feels so close and yet denied?" She asked me, her voice carrying the weight of the unseen danger she had faced.

As she continued, her recounting of the events painted a vivid picture of fear and uncertainty. "With trembling hands, I swept my torchlight across the surrounding foliage. But there was nothing to be seen. Yet, despite the absence of any visible threat, I couldn't shake the feeling of being watched, of unseen eyes following my every move. And then, just as I approached a large cashew tree, I saw it—a shadowy figure lurking in the darkness," she said, her voice barely above a whisper. "It's features were obscured by the dim glow of my torch, but its eyes reflected the light, glowing eerily in the night."

Time seemed to stand still as Shalini described the tense encounter. "With a heart pounding in my chest, I slowly began to retreat," she continued, her words echoing the fear that gripped her. "My mind reeled with fear and uncertainty as I hurried back to my aunt's side, breathless and shaken."

Her story left me with a sense of unease, the lingering presence of the darkness and its secrets hanging in the air.

"The next morning brought a grim discovery," Shalini continued, her voice heavy with sorrow. "Rocky's lifeless body lay near the tree, his remains ravaged by some unknown predator. The sight filled me with terror, realising how close I had been to the creature responsible for his demise. Was it a leopard, a tiger, or something else entirely? The uncertainty gnawed at me, haunting my thoughts for months to come."

She paused, the memory of that morning still vivid in her mind. "Despite the passage of time, the memory of those glowing eyes lingered, a constant reminder of the darkness that lurked just beyond the safety of our home."

Shalini's expression turned sombre as she recounted the events that followed. "But little did I know that another harrowing encounter awaited me, one that would forever alter the course of my life."

****

Shalini's voice trembled as she began recounting that fateful night. "Flashback to an ordinary night, much like any other," she started. "I carried out my routine task of securing our cow in the cowshed. The familiar darkness surrounded me as I moved by muscle memory, the soft shuffling of hooves and the creaking of wooden beams echoing in the silence."

"It was late, well past 11:00 PM," she continued, her voice growing heavier with each passing moment. "But the task was one I had performed countless times before, never suspecting that it would lead to a brush with danger. Exhaustion weighed heavily on my eyelids as I completed the last task before retiring to bed. An hour passed, maybe two."

"Suddenly, a deafening roar shattered the peacefulness of the night," Shalini recounted, her eyes wide with fear. "A massive tiger had crept into the shed, feasting on the very animal I had tethered. In my drowsy state, I mistook the tiger for my gentle cow.

"As the village awoke to the terrifying reality, panic swept through the air. I was frozen with fear," Shalini admitted, her heart racing at the memory. "How could I possibly face such a formidable predator? The tiger's gaze locked onto mine, and for a moment, I was completely paralysed by those glowing eyes.

"Amidst the panic, the villagers hastily gathered, devising a plan to save me and themselves from the ferocious predator. Stones were hurled at the tiger, attempting to drive it away. The struggle intensified as the tiger fought back, determined to hold its ground.

"Suddenly, with a burst of strength, the tiger managed to snap the pole to which it was tethered. Chaos ensued as the majestic creature swiftly vanished into the nearby forest, disappearing with the rope still entangled around it."

Upon hearing Shalini's tale, I couldn't shake the feeling that there was more to her story than mere luck. Why had the tiger remained strangely docile as she tied the rope around its neck? Could it have been sated after its feast, slipping into a deep slumber? Was Shalini destined to become the local hero, or was it simply a stroke of luck?

****

After recounting the incident, Shalini opened up about the aftermath, revealing the true impact of her newfound fame. The tale of her encounter with the tiger sparked a wave of fascination and intrigue, transforming her into a local legend overnight. Her bravery in taming the tiger captured imaginations and inspired awe among all who heard it. However, Shalini soon realised that fame was a double-edged sword.

The village, initially enraptured by her story, began to flock to her humble abode, eager for a first-hand account of the legendary tiger-tamer. Shalini, though grateful for the attention, found herself becoming a reluctant hostess, serving tea and snacks to the steady stream of visitors. With each retelling of her tale, the once-thrilling event began to feel like a monotonous routine, wearing away at her spirit.

As the initial excitement waned, life began to return to normal for Shalini. The village's fascination with her extraordinary encounter slowly faded, replaced by the routine of everyday life. Yet, amidst the whispers of luck and divine intervention, Shalini couldn't shake the feeling that her connection to the extraordinary ran deeper than mere chance.

(Artistic Impression)

As time went on, the villagers spoke less frequently of the incident, but the whispers of the extraordinary lingered, leaving Shalini with a sense that her life had been touched by something greater—a connection to the mysteries that lurked within the depths of the forest.

4. THEY COME BACK

After a decade, Umanath returned to his ancestral home. The demands of his work and city life had kept him occupied, leaving little time for travel. As a student, he used to visit the house every summer vacation, creating cherished memories.

During this Diwali, Umanath's uncle couldn't make it due to ill health. Hence, his mother took on the responsibility of lighting the diyas in the house. With his father busy, Umanath accompanied his mother on the journey.

As they bumped along the village roads, Umanath's gaze drifted over the landscape, searching for signs of the past amidst the present. His heart fluttered with a mixture of excitement and apprehension, wondering if the familiar sights that once filled his childhood with joy still existed in their former glory.

The farms, once lush and abundant with life, now appeared weathered and worn, yet still exuding a sense of resilience. Mango and coconut trees swayed in the breeze, their branches heavy with fruit, a testament to the enduring cycle of nature.

Amidst the fields, he spotted the familiar shapes of grazing animals: cows lazily chewing cud, goats bounding playfully, and chickens pecking at the ground. Their presence reassured him, grounding him in the comforting familiarity of rural life.

****

Two days before their arrival, the house had been thoroughly cleaned since the servants would be on leave for Diwali.

Nestled amidst acres of coconut and mango farms, the house stood grand and inviting. Umanath's heart raced with anticipation as they approached the familiar gates of his ancestral home. The rustling leaves and the scent of earth mingled with memories of his carefree childhood days. As they stepped out of the car, Umanath's eyes swept over the sprawling estate, taking in every detail that seemed both familiar and had changed over time.

The once vibrant gardens now seemed overgrown, with wildflowers reclaiming their space amidst the coconut and mango trees. The pathways that he used to run along now seemed narrower, as if time had shrunk them to fit the confines of memory. Yet the essence of the place remained, echoing with the laughter of past summers.

Upon entering the house, Umanath was greeted by the familiar scent of incense and the coolness of polished stone floors. Shadows danced on the walls as sunlight filtered through the intricately carved windows, casting patterns reminiscent of childhood games. He felt a rush of nostalgia as he walked through the corridors, each corner holding echoes of laughter and whispered secrets. Umanath vividly recalled how he and his cousins would play hide and seek in the dark corridors, adding a sense of adventure to their visits.

****

Umanath felt utterly worn out from the rough journey along the village roads. Spotting a comfy leather couch on the veranda, he plopped down with a sigh, his body craving rest. He could almost feel his eyelids drooping, heavy with exhaustion.

But even in his fatigue, Umanath couldn't help but notice how lively his mother seemed in their old home.

"Umanath, will you come with me to the grocery shop? I need oil and other stuff, plus I want to visit the temple. It'll bring back memories," she chirped.

"Mom, I'm really tired from the journey. If you don't mind, I'd like to take a proper rest," Umanath replied wearily.

"Okay, you go ahead and rest. I've left some cookies and milk on the table for you," his mother said, grabbing an empty grocery bag and a small oil jar before heading towards the market.

Umanath watched his mother until she disappeared near the gate, which was about thirty metres away, and then he fell asleep on the couch.

When he woke, the gentle patter of rain filled the air. Umanath's grandmother sat peacefully on an armchair, gazing out at the farm. Upon seeing him, she greeted him, "Awake now, dear? You must be tired after such a long journey."

(Artistic Impression Of Grandma)

"The roads here are terrible, grandma," Umanath responded, still groggy.

"Your mother left some milk and biscuits on the table. Go and have them," his grandmother suggested kindly.

"Yes, Grandma, she told me before she left. I'll enjoy them," Umanath replied, making his way to the dining table to savour the treats.

His grandmother slowly walked along the long corridor, aided by her walking stick. Umanath playfully remarked, "Grandma, you seem to be getting younger every day."

She chuckled and retorted, "Well, since you young folks are here, my radiance is shining through."

Umanath strolled alongside his grandmother, engaging in conversation about his work and city life. Eventually, they settled on the veranda, with his grandmother comfortably seated in her rocking chair while Umanath sat on the floor, gazing out at the farm. The rain had subsided, creating a cosy atmosphere.

"It has been so quiet in this house without the servants during their Diwali vacation. Today, with you all here, there is finally some liveliness. I'm delighted," his grandmother remarked with a smile.

"Yes, grandma, the weather outside is quite dull as well," Umanath replied, enjoying the tranquilly.

Just then, they spotted Umanath's mother returning through the gate.

"Look, your mom is back. The rose apples are exceptionally delicious this time. Have some before you leave," his grandmother suggested cheerfully.

Before Umanath could respond, his mother approached. Observing him sitting on the veranda, she asked, "How are you feeling now? Refreshed?"

"I'm feeling alright, mom. Grandma was just mentioning the rose apples," Umanath replied.

His mother smiled warmly and said, "Ah, so you still remember. Before you arrived, your grandmother used to handpick and save the most delicious rose apples just for you."

In that moment, a jolt of shock coursed through Umanath's body. He suddenly remembered that his grandmother had passed away two years ago, and he had been unable to attend her funeral due to being abroad. He turned to look at the empty armchair, realising that no one was there.

Was it all a dream? Had he been hallucinating? If it was a dream, Umanath thought, he couldn't help but be grateful for such a wondrous and indelible experience. It felt like the best Diwali gift he could ever receive—a cherished encounter with his grandmother's presence, even if it existed only in his subconscious.

6. THE ENEGMATIC ILLUSIONS OF KAJUKOPPA

As Ramesh peddled through the isolated and eerie surroundings of Kajukoppa on his bicycle, he couldn't shake off the fear that gripped him. The area was partially deserted, with dense cashew trees resembling a wild jungle. There was no habitation nearby except for a peculiar house belonging to Gulabi. Gulabi herself was a striking figure, standing at an astonishing height of over 6 feet, an uncommon sight in a country where the average height for women was 5.2 feet.

Ramesh had always dreaded passing through Kajukoppa, especially at night. The place had an air of mystery and strange tales surrounding it. He vividly remembered catching a glimpse of Gulabi one night, standing near her house, which had terrified him even more. But today, with his groceries securely stowed in his bicycle basket, he rode cautiously.

Earlier in the day, he had visited the market, only to find a few essential items missing. This led him on a search through various shops, causing a delay in his journey back home. What hurt him more was missing out on the evening drama show near Belambar Beach. His friends had raved about it, describing thrilling scenes of kings in combat and more.

The dimly lit road only deepened Ramesh's unease as he pedalled on, silently reciting prayers to various gods in his mind, hoping to distract himself until he left Kajukoppa behind. However, a kilometre felt endless, stretching his nerves thin.

****

As he rode, Ramesh's eyes widened in disbelief at the sight of a horse-drawn cart approaching from the opposite direction. It was a bizarre sight since such carts had become obsolete long ago. The cart, painted an eerie white and adorned with royal markings, gave off an ancient vibe. Even more unsettling was the charioteer, dressed in peculiar garments reminiscent of servants from bygone eras.

As their paths crossed, the cart driver locked eyes with Ramesh, sending him a chilling smile that made his blood run cold. Driven by fear, Ramesh peddled as fast as he could, but his panic caused him to veer off the road and crash into a rock. Groceries flew in all directions as he tumbled to the ground, paralysed and unable to move.

Lying there helplessly, Ramesh's gaze turned to the sky, feeling abandoned by fate.

****

Fortunately, Gulabi happened to witness Ramesh's fall. With a sense of urgency, she and her father rushed to Ramesh's aid, gathering his scattered groceries and guiding him to their house for safety.

Although Ramesh had always prayed to avoid encountering Gulabi at night, she unexpectedly became his saviour on this occasion.

Gulabi and her father helped him to their house and eased him onto an old coir-string cot. Ramesh remained stunned, unable to speak, as he took in his surroundings—an ancient tiled house adorned with weathered posters. Gulabi sat by his side while her father gently tended to his minor bruises. The unease he felt persisted, intensifying with each passing moment.

As Ramesh gathered his courage to share his unsettling encounter with Gulabi and her father, their expressions softened into concern.

Sensing his distress, Gulabi took the lead, her voice calm and reassuring. "Such illusions are not uncommon in this area," she began, her words aimed at easing his fear. "I have witnessed them many times before. Sometimes it's a tiger seemingly running

35

through the night or an old man strolling in the darkness."

Her gentle reassurance aimed to comfort Ramesh, letting him know that what he experienced was not unheard of in Kajukoppa. As Gulabi spoke, her father nodded in agreement, his eyes showing understanding. Together, they sought to ease Ramesh's troubled mind with their shared knowledge of the strange phenomena that lingered in their village.

Intrigued and still bewildered, Ramesh probed further: "Illusions? Why do they occur in this area? Even my mother would never let me travel through here at night. I always thought it was because of the nearby cemetery. But these kinds of illusions?"

Gulabi's father took a moment before responding, delving into the stories passed down through their family's generations. "My ancestors have spoken of these illusions for ages. Suddenly, they would see an old man appearing, or a tiger lurking in the bushes, or even strange birds."

"But who creates these illusions?" Ramesh inquired, his voice quivering slightly, as Gulabi's father offered him a glass of water.

"My ancestors believed that a peculiar creature had dwelled in these forests for centuries," Gulabi's father explained. "They spoke of an animal, similar to a monkey with large eyes, that possesses an incredibly long lifespan. This creature has the ability to capture memories, like photographs, and randomly project them back onto its surroundings. It has accumulated a vast collection of memories over the years, which it projects, resulting in the sightings of bullock carts and tigers. Some of these illusions may have occurred years ago."

Gulabi's father continued, sharing another intriguing ancestral tale. "In a time when fear gripped the hearts of many villagers, they sought the aid of the local landlord. He, in turn, commissioned hunters to track down and capture the elusive creature. Despite the modest size of Kajukoppa, the hunters returned empty-handed, unable to claim the bountiful reward on offer."

Eager to know more, Ramesh leaned forward, his curiosity burning. "Has your family ever encountered this creature?" he asked, his eyes fixed on Gulabi's father.

Reflecting on his 70 years of life, Gulabi's father recounted a rare and personal encounter. "One early morning, as I ventured into the woods to gather firewood, I came face-to-face with the creature. It darted into the underbrush, staring at me with its uncanny eyes. Its gaze seemed to flash a light upon me before vanishing into dense vegetation. That was the first and only time I had ever encountered such a creature. Perhaps, in some later years, it may have projected my own image as well."

With the ancestral stories and personal experiences shared, Ramesh's understanding of the strange phenomena in Kajukoppa deepened. The village held onto a long-kept secret, tied to the existence of a mysterious creature capable of playing tricks on people's minds with illusions.

(Artistic Impression Of The Creature)

As Ramesh lay in Gulabi's house, his physical wounds gradually healing, he couldn't help but wonder about the countless hidden tales concealed within the dense forests and mist-laden hills of Kajukoppa, waiting to be discovered by those brave enough to venture into the unknown.

6. THE SADHUS WORDS

Amma, my grandmother, despite her rural upbringing, possessed a unique and commendable habit. In her household of ten, she consistently prepared enough food for twelve people. She always set aside extra portions for those in need, a practice she maintained year-round due to the frequent visits of hungry people knocking at her door. Her conviction was grounded in the belief that addressing hunger held greater spiritual significance than unending hours of prayer. Consequently, she devoted herself to ensuring no one left her doorstep with an empty stomach. This tradition had been passed down through generations in her family.

Amma's storytelling had a unique power to transport me to a different time and place, and I cherished those moments with her. It was in these stories that I found a deep sense of belonging and a connection to the generations that had come before me. And so, even though I had heard the story countless times, I knew that I would ask Amma to tell it again, and again, and again.

I chuckled as I settled beside Amma, feeling a bit restless. "Amma, could you tell me one of your stories again? The one about the Sadhu, perhaps?"

Amma's eyes twinkled, and she patted my head lovingly. "Ah, you never tire of that one, do you? But, of course, I'll tell it to you again." She took a deep breath, ready to transport me into another world with her words.

"Amma," I said, sitting at her feet, "tell me more about the Sadhu from Kashmir. What did he look like? How did he convey his hunger?"

Amma's eyes sparkled with nostalgia as she began to recount the tale. "Well, he was a tall man with a flowing white beard . His clothes were tattered, and his eyes held a deep wisdom. He didn't speak our language, but his gestures were clear. He'd put his hands together near his mouth, mimicking eating, and then he'd rub his stomach with a look of hunger."

I leaned in closer, captivated by her storytelling. "And what did you do when you saw him?"

Amma's voice softened. "It was around three in the afternoon, and our food supply was running low. But I couldn't bear to see him hungry. So, I decided to start from scratch and cook a meal for him. I knew that even if we had just enough for our family, we couldn't send him away with an empty stomach."

I could almost smell the aroma of the meal cooking in her kitchen as she continued. "I made him rice and dal, some vegetables we had, and a chapati. It wasn't much, but his eyes lit up with gratitude when I served it to him. He ate with contentment, as if it was the best meal he ever had."

I couldn't help but smile at the image of the Sadhu enjoying Amma's humble meal. "And then he gave you that blessing?"

Amma nodded, her eyes misty with the memory. "Yes, my dear. After he finished eating, he looked at me and said, 'May you never face a shortage of rice in your home.' It was a simple blessing, but it carried such weight."

"As the story goes," Amma began, "the Sadhu's blessing worked like magic. You see, not long after that encounter, a harsh drought descended upon Honavar. It was a tough time for everyone. The wealthy were importing rice from far-off places, and those less fortunate were going to bed with empty stomachs, night after night."

My curiosity was piqued. "What about our family, Amma? How did we fare during this drought?"

Amma's eyes glinted with a mixture of nostalgia and amazement. "Well, my dear, that's where your grandfather's unique habits came into play."

"Grandpa's habits? You mean his stockpiling?" I asked, remembering the sacks of rice and other supplies he used to collect.

"Yes, exactly," Amma nodded. "You see, at the beginning of each year, your grandfather would gather a substantial reserve of resources. He stockpiled twelve sacks of rice, each weighing a whopping 100 kilograms. And that wasn't all; he had caches of jaggery, and when the time was right, he even stored pumpkins. It was all part of his plan to secure our family's survival for at least a year in case of unforeseen misfortune."

I couldn't help but be impressed by Grandpa's foresight. "But, Amma, storing all that food must have been quite a challenge, right?"

Amma chuckled softly. "Oh, you have no idea, my dear. Keeping everything in good shape was indeed a challenge. Ants sometimes found their way to the rice, and the dampness could spoil some of the supplies. I used to tell your grandfather that we could always buy food from the store when we needed it, but he had a different way of thinking."

I leaned back, considering the contrast between our household and the rest of the town. "So, while everyone else was struggling and some were even surviving on wild yams, we had this abundance of rice?"

Amma nodded proudly. "Yes, that's right. While a significant portion of the townspeople had to resort to consuming wild yams to ward off hunger, we remained untouched by the drought. That blessing from the Sadhu and your grandfather's unusual practices, they worked together like a charm to shield our family from the impact of the crisis."

As Amma finished her story, I couldn't help but admire the wisdom and foresight of my grandparents. Their unique practices had not only saved our family from the ravages of the drought but also left a lasting legacy of resilience and compassion.

(Artistic Impression Of Sadhu)

7. THE WHISPERS OF HEGDE HOUSE

In the heart of a remote Indian village nestled within the Ankola Taluka region, Hegde House commanded both reverence and trepidation. Amidst the sprawling coconut groves, this venerable mansion was a living relic of times long past, where history whispered its tales through the rustling leaves of the coconut trees. When night descended, and the moonlight filtered through the dense canopy, it painted eerie patterns on the ground, conjuring an otherworldly atmosphere that defied the boundaries of reality.

Despite the modern upgrades that had infiltrated its interior through renovations, Hegde House clung stubbornly to its historical roots. The red oxide floors bore the marks of countless footsteps, the faded tapestries on the walls murmured tales now forgotten, and the wooden staircase had supported the weight of generations. Dimly lit lamps waged a losing battle against the ever-shifting shadows that danced upon the walls. Even on the hottest of days, an unnatural chill seemed to hang in the air. Time had caressed the house with its gentle hand, preserving it in a perpetual state of antiquity, as if the secrets of the Hegde family were an indelible part of its very soul.

The author's uncle, a curious soul drawn to the mystique of the place, had once been a guest within its walls. Years later, he would regale the author with stories that added another layer of intrigue to the house's mystique. As he sat in the shadows of the coconut groves, eating a mango, a voice pierced the stillness of the night.

"Can you give me some lime, sir, please?" implored a villager who ventured towards the imposing Hegde House. His request, though seemingly innocuous, required him to tread about 100 metres into the heart of the estate, an unusual journey for a simple request like chewing beetle leaf.

The patriarch of the Hegde family, a man whose features bore the etchings of countless years, stepped forward. A faint smile graced his lips as he posed an unexpected question: "Have you taken anything from our farm?"

The villager's eyes widened, caught off guard by the inquiry. After a moment's hesitation, he confessed, "I apologise, sir. Last night, on my way home, I chanced upon a fallen coconut on the edge of your farm. I took it and used it in our curry. Since then, I've been plagued by relentless bouts of vomiting."

The old man smiled, seeming to understand the situation. "It's okay," he said kindly. Then he reached for a lime from a nearby basket and handed it to the villager. "Just remember, don't take anything from our farm without asking. There are more secrets on our farm than you can imagine."

As the villager expressed his gratitude and hastened away, he couldn't escape the lingering curiosity that the encounter had ignited.

****

The author's uncle, now steeped in the allure of Hegde House's mysteries, ventured further into its enigma. Approaching the old patriarch, who had overseen the household for generations, he inquired about the unusual exchange.

The old man's eyes sparkled with timeless wisdom as he beckoned for the visitor to follow him. "Come," he invited, leading the way to a hut-like structure that resembled a rustic temple nestled within the estate. The uncle followed, captivated by the unfolding narrative.

Arriving at the temple, the old man gestured towards a wooden idol within—a deity carved from ancient wood. The figure bore a stern countenance, and it was adorned with offerings of fruits and flowers.

"Our forebears established this temple," the old man began, "dedicated to this wooden deity. It is said to be the guardian of our farm. When someone steals something from our land, they get sick, just like the villager who needed the lime. The sickness doesn't go away until they eat something given by the owner of the farm."

The uncle listened closely, fascinated by this strange belief. "So, this god made the villager sick, and that's why he needed the lime?"

The old man nodded. "Precisely. It's a tradition steeped in generations of history. We hold a deep reverence for our land, and this deity ensures that those who unlawfully take from it are reminded of their actions until they reconcile with their wrongdoing."

Time passed, and the stories of Hegde House and its traditions spread through the village. The villagers started calling the wooden god "The Bhoota of Hegde House." That means "The Ghost of Hegde House" in their language. People respected it, but they also felt a little scared of it.

The author's uncle, now fully caught up in the mysteries of Hegde House, couldn't stop himself from being curious. He asked the old man, "Has anyone in the village ever seen this ghost? Or any strange things around here?"

The old man's eyes sparkled with wisdom and something deeper. He leaned closer to the visitor and whispered, "Many people say they've seen the Bhoota's appearance. Sometimes, during quiet nights or when the moon is shining strangely, a few have spotted a ghostly figure near the temple."

He paused for a moment, carefully choosing his words, and then continued, "But the Bhoota doesn't show itself to just anyone. It's a guardian, and it only appears to those who know the secrets and traditions of the Hegde family. Its appearances are both a blessing and a warning. It reminds us of the special bond between our land and its protectors."

The old man drew a deep breath and went on, "I was around 27 or 28 at the time, I reckon. After the harvest, I loaded sacks of grain onto our bullock cart and journeyed to Ankola to sell our produce. In those days, the tehsildar had to inspect the grain's quality, and he was running late, prolonging the paperwork.

"By the time I sold the grain and embarked on the journey back, night had already descended. Rain poured relentlessly, and my body began to ache, soon escalating to a fever that gripped me. I struggled on the way back; the bullock cart ride took hours, and the roads were far from the well-paved ones we have today. It was a challenging journey."

The old man's voice grew softer as he continued, "By the time I reached our gate, it was well past midnight, though I couldn't be certain as I didn't have a watch. The rain was still falling, and the lantern on the bullock cart had been extinguished during the journey. I knew that I couldn't bring the cart any further into the property, so I tied up the bulls outside. It's quite a walk to reach the house—over a hundred metres or more. And on that rainy night, walking without light was dangerous. I couldn't even call out for the servants because my throat itched and my voice had faded. I was left standing at the gate, shivering from both the fever and the cold rain."

The old man continued, "But then, suddenly, a lantern appeared, floating in the air. It was pitch dark, and I couldn't see the person holding it, and if there was a person at all. What I could make out was a silhouette-like figure. I called out, 'Is it Ramu?' No reply. 'Is it Ganpu?' Again, no response. I tried half a dozen servants' names, but not a single soul answered. As I approached the light of the house, the lantern dispersed suddenly. I couldn't tell if it had gone out or if it had simply vanished. I searched the area but found no one. The next day, I asked all the servants, and none of them claimed to have carried the lantern. It remains a mystery to this day whether it was something else that carried the lantern to show me the path. That's the only time I ever witnessed such an occurrence," the old man concluded, his voice tinged with a mix of wonder and uncertainty.

Uncle sat in silence for a moment, absorbing the strangeness of the story. It seemed that the mysteries of Hegde House were not confined to the Bhoota alone; there were other inexplicable events that defied explanation. As he gazed at the old man, he couldn't help but feel that the enigmatic aura of the place extended beyond the stories and legends and into the very fabric of its existence.

****

As time flowed forward to the present day, a fateful event occurred that would further entwine the mysteries of Hegde House with the passage of time. A powerful lightning strike struck the grass hut that had housed the ancient idol of the Bhoota, reducing it to ashes. The once-protective sanctuary for the guardian spirit was no more.

(Artistic Impression of Lantern)

In the aftermath of this lightning strike, an eerie change seemed to sweep over the Hegde farm. Incidents of theft and unexplained occurrences became increasingly common. Tools would vanish overnight, and the livestock would act strangely, as if spooked by an unseen presence. The old man, now a grandfather, could only narrate the tales of the Bhoota and its traditions to his curious grandchildren.

The grandchildren of the old man were eager to preserve the legacy of the Bhoota and the traditions of Hegde House. They felt a deep connection to their ancestral home, its mysteries, and the guardian spirit that had been an integral part of their family's history. As they listened to their grandfather's stories, they couldn't help but wonder if there was a way to rekindle the presence of the Bhoota and restore the protective aura that had once safeguarded their land.

Uncle, though captivated by the tales he'd heard, couldn't help but question their authenticity. Were these narratives and stories intentionally crafted to instil psychological fear and safeguard the farms? Or was there indeed an otherworldly entity that watched over the Hegde land?

In the end, the truth remained elusive, veiled in the mists of time and the uncertainties of human belief. Hegde House stood as a silent sentinel, guarding its enigmatic secrets, leaving each generation to ponder the mysteries that shrouded its ancient halls.

8. THE GIANTS ON THE ISLAND

Anil poured the steaming tea from his crimson Milton thermos and extended it to the old man, whose weathered face softened into a grateful smile; it was just the warmth he craved on such a chilly night. With paper cups in hand, they settled onto the cold cement seats, gazing out over the expansive beach beneath the moonlit sky.

Every day, without fail, Anil followed the rhythm of his routine. From dawn till dusk, he dutifully fulfilled his role at the bank, serving as the trusted agent for the Pigmy Deposit Scheme. Yet, as the sun dipped below the horizon, his true passion ignited. Evenings were reserved for his craft, delicately carving intricate statues of diverse deities from blocks of wood, which he then peddled to local shops, adding a modest but meaningful supplement to his income.

However, after dinner, Anil allotted himself an hour or two for relaxation. He sauntered along the beach, far from the hustle and bustle of tourists, often encountering only the occasional fisherman returning under the veil of night. Stretching for miles, the beach remained largely untouched, a sanctuary of solitude for Anil. The cool breeze, laced with the scent of sea salt, offered him a soothing respite from the day's toils. It felt as though his brain was bathed in an extra dose of dopamine in this serene environment.

In recent nights, Anil found himself accompanied by the old man, who would join him halfway through his solitary walks. Though Anil had never ventured to the other side of the hill where the old man lived, their nightly encounters had forged a gentle bond between them.

Tonight, following his usual routine, Anil wandered along the beach, accompanied by the soft melodies emanating from his portable radio. Tuning in to the evening news, he sought topics for discussion with the old man he'd grown accustomed to meeting.

Anil strolled along the beach, guided by the soft glow of the moon reflecting off the water. Suddenly, he felt a chill of apprehension as he spotted a massive shape looming in the dark ahead.

Drawing closer, his heart pounded with a mixture of fear and fascination as he realised the enormity of the creature before him—a colossal turtle, its silhouette outlined against the moonlit horizon. The rhythmic sound of its flippers thrashing the sand filled the air, amplifying the intensity of the moment. Anil followed, his eyes locked onto the creature's immense shell, which bore the marks of countless journeys through the unforgiving depths of the ocean.

With a grace that belied its colossal size, the turtle reached the water's edge, its massive form silhouetted against the moonlit waves. Anil stood transfixed, his breath caught in his throat, as the creature turned its gaze towards him, its eyes gleaming like orbs of polished onyx in the dim light.

For a fleeting moment, time seemed to stand still as Anil and the turtle locked eyes, two beings from different worlds connected by a shared moment of awe and wonder. Then, with a powerful surge of movement, the turtle plunged into the water with a resounding splash, disappearing beneath the surface in a swirl of foam and bubbles.

As the last echoes of its departure faded into the night, Anil remained rooted to the spot, his mind awash with a whirlwind of emotions. "What a magnificent creature," he whispered to himself, unable to tear his gaze away from the spot where the turtle had vanished. "If only I had a camera," he lamented, imagining the breath-taking image he could have captured.

With a heavy heart, Anil tore himself away from the shoreline and continued on his journey, the memory of the encounter with the colossal turtle etched into his mind forevermore.

Today, Anil brought along some paper cups and a thermos of tea to share with the old man. As they settled in, cradling their cups of warmth, Anil recounted the enchanting encounter with the colossal turtle that graced the shores of their secluded haven.

"You're fortunate indeed, Anil," the old man remarked, his weathered features softening with nostalgia as he savoured his tea. "I've witnessed a few turtles along these shores over the years, but one of such colossal proportions is truly a sight to behold—a once-in-a-lifetime experience, I dare say."

"Have you ever encountered any such once-in-a-lifetime sights?" Anil inquired eagerly, his curiosity piqued.

The old man's smile widened at the question, and he began to recollect his memories. "Ah, I've often wished to share this tale, but it's one that few believe," he started, his voice carrying the weight of years gone by. "In my youth, when these hills were dense with forests unlike today, my father and I frequented this place. Leopard-spotted deer sightings were common occurrences back then, and even now, one might catch a glimpse of them from time to time. But amidst those familiar sights, there was one encounter that remains etched in my mind—a sighting of true giants."

"Giants?" Anil echoed, his attention fully captured as he hastily consumed his tea, eager to hear the story unfold.

"Yes, you see those caves out there," the old man gestured, pointing his weathered finger towards the hills on the nearby island.

There, nestled amidst the dense foliage, lay ancient caves. "No one ventures to those islands much these days; they're shrouded in thick forest," he continued, his tone carrying a hint of mystery. "Once a year, there's a small festival held at the foot of those hills, where the old tribal gods are revered. But aside from that occasion, few dare to tread those paths."

The old man's voice took on a reverent tone as he recounted his tale. "Once, many years ago, I sat on this very spot with my father," he began, his gaze drifting towards the smooth boulders that once occupied the place where they now sat upon cement seats. "It was late at night, around ten o'clock, and the full moon bathed the entrance of the cave in its ethereal glow, much like tonight."

He paused, as if transported back to that moment. "Suddenly, a deep, resonant howling echoed through the night, sending shivers down our spines. We searched the surroundings, our hearts pounding, until our eyes fell upon the caves. There, illuminated by the moonlight, stood two colossal figures—giants, we realized. Towering at least nine to ten feet tall, they moved with an otherworldly grace, occasionally emitting haunting sounds. Their muscular forms resembled those of humans, but their size was beyond comprehension. And in the moonlight, their fur appeared to be a shade of brownish fur."

Anil listened intently, captivated by the old man's tale, his imagination weaving vivid images of the mysterious encounter.

The old man's narrative continued, each word imbued with a sense of awe and wonder. "The giants were completely bare, except for hides covering their lower torsos," he elaborated. "One of them wielded a massive log-like stick in his hand, a weapon or perhaps a tool of their own making. We watched in stunned silence as he climbed top of that boulder, lifting his head to the moonlit sky, and emitted a resounding howl—a call, it seemed, to others of his kind who might lurk in the shadows of the forest."

Anil interjected with a note of scepticism, his voice tinged with curiosity. "I've heard of the Cave Man, or the early human ancestor Gigantopithecus," he remarked thoughtfully, "but as far as I know, they went extinct long before our time. How is it possible that you encountered them?"

The old man nodded in agreement, his expression thoughtful as he considered Anil's words. "Indeed, it seems unlikely that both of us could have experienced the same hallucination simultaneously," he conceded. "My father, too, bore witness to that extraordinary sight."

He paused, a contemplative look in his eyes, before continuing, "Sometimes, I can't help but wonder if nature itself acts as a vast repository, a photograph of sorts, storing the visuals and sounds of generations past. And perhaps, under certain conditions, when the chemical processes align as they did hundreds of years ago, these stored memories are projected back to us, allowing us to glimpse things that once were."

(Artistic Impression Of The Giant)

"After that singular encounter, every time I return to this place, I find myself drawn to those caves, searching for any sign of those enigmatic giants," the old man reflected wistfully. "Yet, despite my repeated visits, they never graced my sight again."

Anil nodded, absorbing the old man's words with a sense of wonder. The mystery surrounding the giants lingered in the air, leaving an indelible mark on their shared memories of that fateful encounter.

After bidding farewell to the old man, Anil found himself alone once more, his thoughts lingering on the tale he had just heard. Casting one last glance towards the caves and the boulder nearby, he couldn't shake the feeling of intrigue that had taken hold of him.

As he made his way home, his footsteps tracing the familiar path along the muddy road, Anil's eyes caught sight of something peculiar—footprints. They resembled those of a human, yet appeared weathered and worn, as if imprinted by beings of great strength and stature. A shiver ran down his spine as he contemplated the possibility of the creatures the old man had described, wondering if they still roamed the hidden corners of the island, unseen by human eyes.

9. NO SHORTCUTS

Seated near the temple, Mukund found himself engulfed in reflections on the wastefulness of his youth. With only a fifth-grade education, he now finds himself in his early 50s, grappling with regret. Time had slipped through his fingers like sand, leaving him pondering the swift passage of three decades. Scraping by on the meagre proceeds from the family's leased ancestral farm and taking refuge in his ageing parents' home, Mukund found himself possessing little else.

Memories flooded back of carefree days spent idling away time with friends near the schoolyard or lounging at the betel leaf shop, indulging in light-hearted banter at the expense of passers-by. In those moments, the weight of responsibility or the importance of investing in his future were scarcely registered. Neither his academic pursuits nor his entrepreneurial ventures received the attention they deserved.

As time ambled on, Mukund watched as his friends embarked on the journey of marriage and family life, leaving him behind in a state of increasing isolation. His own parents faced mounting difficulties in finding a suitable match for him, with his lack of financial stability proving to be a formidable barrier. Mukund harboured the desire for a fair bride, yet his empty pockets deterred any prospective suitors. With each passing day, the prospect of matrimony faded further from reach, until hope itself seemed a distant memory by the time he crossed the threshold of 48. Now, as he gazes upon his friends and their grown children, Mukund is confronted with the stark reality of his own stagnation. The past three decades have yielded little in terms of tangible progress or personal achievement. Even the modest income he manages to eke out owes itself more to the charity of relatives than to any genuine effort on his part.

Mukund's existence had dwindled into a monotonous routine devoid of ambition, aspiration, or challenge. In the absence of familial responsibilities, Mukund found solace and companionship in Govind, a fellow widower who, unlike him, had seen his children off into their own lives. Together, they formed an unlikely bond.

Their days were filled with fervent discussions on the state of the nation, delving deep into the intricacies of politics and governance. In their exchanges, they explored alternate paths that the government could have taken, envisioning a brighter future for their country had different decisions been made.

In each other, they discovered a source of companionship and camaraderie that helped to fill the void left by the absence of family, offering a glimmer of hope.

****

One day, amidst their lively political discourse at the betel shop, a curious interruption arrived in the form of a fortune teller. Mukund couldn't resist a joke, playfully ribbing Govind about the eccentricity of seeking predictions from such a figure. Yet, with time to spare and perhaps a hint of curiosity themselves, they decided to indulge the fortune teller and learn what fate might have in store for Mukund.

As the fortune teller observed Mukund and gauged the time of day in the betel shop, a sense of mystery hung in the air. With a solemn demeanour, the fortune teller began to speak, his words carrying an air of prophetic certainty.

"You, Mukund, are bound by the threads of destiny," he intoned, his voice carrying a weight of authority. "Your past may not have been as prosperous as it could have been, but I sense a change on the horizon. A stroke of luck is destined to find its way to you—a fortune of sorts, be it through a stroke of luck in the form of a lottery win or the discovery of hidden treasure. It awaits you, poised to alter the course of your life."

Amused by the fortune teller's predictions, Mukund couldn't help but scoff at the notion of suddenly stumbling upon a windfall of fortune. "Lottery winnings, eh? We've been trying our luck for ages with no success," he quipped, shaking his head in disbelief. With a dismissive wave and a handful of coins, Mukund bid the fortune teller farewell, his laughter trailing behind him as they departed the betel shop.

(Artistic Impression Of Fortune Teller)

Turning to Govind, Mukund resumed their discussion with a renewed sense of levity. "Imagine relying on a fortune teller who can't even foresee his own fate," he remarked with a grin. With their scepticism intact and their hunger growing, they decided to leave the betel shop behind and head off for lunch, leaving the fortune teller's words behind as nothing more than a fleeting amusement in the tapestry of their day.

****

A few days later, Mukund and Govind set out on a voyage to a temple nestled on an island. Their longing to visit the island had persisted for quite some time, and at last, they stumbled upon the opportune moment to do so.

As they made their return journey, the allure of the island's scenic beauty beckoned to them, enticing them to stray from the beaten path in search of panoramic views of the surrounding waters. Bathed in the golden glow of the setting sun, Mukund's gaze was suddenly drawn to a distinct glint of metal catching the light.

Intrigued, Mukund approached the spot where the sunlight had illuminated a mysterious object partially buried in the earth. With a sense of anticipation coursing through him, Mukund reached down and retrieved the object from its earthen confines. As he brushed away the layers of soil and debris, a gleaming copper disc-shaped object emerged, its surface glinting in the fading light.

With bated breath, Mukund examined the object more closely, his fingers tracing the intricate patterns etched into its surface. Could this be the fabled stroke of luck foretold by the fortune teller—a treasure waiting to be unearthed, hidden in the unlikeliest of places? Sensing the urgency of the situation, he swiftly stowed the disc in his bag and led Govind away from the area.

Curious about their find, Govind queried, "What was that, Mukund?"

Mukund's response was swift and cautious. "Shhh, I'll explain everything later. We cannot discuss it here."

With a shared understanding of the need for secrecy, they continued on their way, the mystery of the disc weighing heavily on their minds as they retreated to a safer location. As they reached Honnavar, Mukund and Govind hurried to a secluded spot. Govind's curiosity couldn't be contained. "Is it a treasure?"

Mukund retrieved the disc from his bag and examined it closely. English inscriptions adorned its surface, but their meaning remained elusive. Determined to uncover its secrets, Mukund washed the disc, revealing its copper brilliance. However, a red seal-like feature presented a new challenge. Mukund struggled to break it open, while Govind, hindered by his age, could only watch.

Following his unsuccessful attempts to breach the seal, Mukund's eyes fell upon a sharp stone situated at the edge of the hillock. With a mix of desperation and resolve, he carried the metal disc to this vantage point and forcefully struck it against the stone. The impact echoed like a thunderclap through the quiet town of Honnavar, sending shockwaves of sound rippling through the serene evening air. The deafening roar shattered the peaceful tranquillity, jolting residents from their evening routines.

For a fleeting moment, time seemed to freeze as the shockwave reverberated throughout the entire town. Birds took flight in a panicked frenzy, their wings beating against the sudden chaos, while windows rattled violently in their frames, as if struggling to contain the force of the explosion. Then, as abruptly as it had begun, the explosion subsided, leaving behind an eerie silence that hung heavy in the air. The stunned residents of Honnavar emerged from their homes, their faces etched with disbelief as they surveyed the aftermath of the tumultuous event.

In the wake of the explosion, the once peaceful evening had been shattered, replaced by a sense of unease and uncertainty. And as the town began to slowly recover from the shock, questions swirled in the air, each one seeking to unravel the mystery of what had transpired on that fateful night.

****

In the evening, Govind found himself hospitalised and under police inquiry. The First Information Report (FIR) detailed the events: "Mukund and Govind residents of Honnavar ventured to the island and discovered a disc-shaped object, believing it to be a treasure. However, unbeknownst to them, it was a World War II-era British mine that had somehow remained intact. When Mukund attempted to break it open against a rock, it detonated, tragically claiming Mukund's life while Govind sustained minor injuries."

10. THE TANTRIC PARADOX

Sudha and her husband stood before the mysterious hut of the tantric, a sense of foreboding settling over them like a heavy fog. The dimly lit hut exuded an unsettling aura, intensified by the overpowering fragrance of jasmine flowers that seemed to choke the air. At the centre of the room loomed a massive statue of a deity, its imposing presence obscured by a thick blanket of flowers, casting eerie shadows that danced in the flickering light. Sudha's gaze shifted to the figure of the tantric, a man in his late 50s with piercing eyes rimmed in kajal, his stoic demeanour sending a chill through her bones as he sat upon his seat. Whispers seemed to emanate from the walls, carrying tales of forgotten rituals and forbidden knowledge, leaving Sudha and her husband gripped with a primal fear.

Sudha's voice quivered as she whispered to her husband, her words barely audible amidst the eerie silence that enveloped them. "I'm scared," she confessed, her grip tightening on his hand as she glanced nervously at the shadowy entrance to the tantrik's hut. "Are you sure we want to go in here?"

(Artistic Impression of Tantrik)

Her husband's expression betrayed a hint of uncertainty, but determination flickered in his eyes as he squeezed her hand reassuringly. "We've come this far," he replied softly. "We have to see this through."

Together, they took a tentative step forward.

****

For Sudha and her husband, the decision weighed heavy on their hearts. It all began with the purchase of a plot near the New Colony in Hubli, where Suresh, Sudha's husband, had set his sights on the coveted corner plot. Their joy knew no bounds when they successfully secured the desired land. Suresh was elated, feeling as if he had stepped into a dream world.

However, their euphoria soon turned to dismay when they attempted to begin construction on their new home, only to find an illegal hut standing in its place. Erected by a tribal family years ago, what was meant to be a temporary shelter had become a permanent fixture.

Despite numerous pleas from the society to vacate the premises, the family adamantly refused. Though the vast majority of the plot lay vacant, the hut encroached upon the garden section, leaving Suresh yearning to rid the land of its obstruction so they could build their envisioned beautiful house.

With the aid of the court and the assistance of the police, Suresh finally succeeded in having the hut residents vacated. Sudha and Suresh stood witness as the eviction unfolded before them. As the woman of the house, Sindhu, approached Sudha, her eyes burning with fury, she unleashed a curse upon her. "I will see how you will enjoy your house," she spat, her voice laced with venom. "You destroyed our hut; I will ensure your peace is destroyed forever." With a reluctant glance at Sudha and a malicious grin in her eyes, the woman was forcibly dragged away by the police, leaving Sudha unsettled by the weight of her curse.

After the unsettling incident, Sudha found herself plagued by an inexplicable sense of suffocation, as if the lingering gaze of Sindhu's eyes continued to haunt her every thought. She couldn't shake the feeling of unease; the weight of the curse was heavy on her conscience. At one point, she confided in her husband, voicing her doubts about their course of action. "Suresh, I think we should have offered them some compensation to leave peacefully without involving the court and the police."

Suresh responded with conviction, his voice tinged with reassurance. "Sudha, you always ponder deeply," he said, his tone resolute. "But this land is rightfully ours; we purchased it fair and square. Once our house is built, our new life will begin, and all this will be behind us."

Yet, despite Suresh's words of assurance, Sudha couldn't shake the lingering sense of dread that gnawed at her heart.

****

A few months after the construction of their beautiful house, Sudha and Suresh found themselves brimming with happiness. The initial days felt like stepping into a luxurious resort, with Sudha meticulously arranging decorations and marvelling at their new abode for hours on end. It was like stepping into a dream world, so much so that Sudha playfully urged Suresh to pinch her to ensure it wasn't just a fantasy.

A few weeks later their troubles started. Each morning, Sudha would venture onto the terrace, only to find a disturbing array of objects left behind: lemons cut and dipped in red liquid, feathers from hens, and mysterious items wrapped in old cloths. Occasionally, she even stumbled upon eerie voodoo dolls, their chests pierced with pins, sending a chill down her spine. Despite her attempts to rationalise these unsettling discoveries, Sudha couldn't shake the feeling of unease that pervaded their once peaceful home.

As the incidents escalated, Sudha found herself descending into a deep depression, haunted by the relentless presence of the mysterious woman, both in her waking life and in her dreams. The unexplained objects left on their terrace at night only added to Sudha's growing sense of unease, while the feeling of being watched intensified, even manifesting as hallucinations.

A shadowy figure seemed to stalk her every move, its presence an ever-looming spectre that refused to dissipate. With each passing day, Sudha's mental state deteriorated, her once tranquil existence shattered by the relentless onslaught of fear and paranoia. Unable to find respite from the relentless torment, Sudha felt as though she were trapped in a waking nightmare from which there was no escape.

Driven by desperation and a newfound belief in the supernatural, Suresh took numerous leaves from his job at the bank and took help from his colleagues to track down the current location of the tribal family's hut. Initially approaching them with stern warnings, Suresh later adopted a gentler approach, appealing to their sense of compassion and understanding. He implored Sindhu, the woman haunting Sudha, to cease her disturbances once and for all.

Despite Suresh's efforts, a resolution remained elusive as both parties' egos clashed in a battle of wills. Sindhu, fuelled by a determination to avenge the eviction from their hut, refused to back down. Threateningly, she claimed to have unleashed the forces of black magic, declaring that they were now in its dark grip with no hope of escape. As tensions escalated and the stakes grew higher, Suresh and Sudha found themselves ensnared in a dangerous game of supernatural warfare, their once peaceful existence now overshadowed by the looming threat of Sindhu's vengeful curses.

Despite Suresh's desperate attempts to seek help for Sudha, including visits to psychologists, her condition continued to deteriorate. She remained plagued by fear, hearing voices, and experiencing unexplained phenomena that no amount of therapy could alleviate. As a last resort, someone suggested that Suresh seek the guidance of the tantric who resided in the hut outside the city. After much deliberation and hesitation, Suresh finally made the decision to seek the tantrik's help. And so, after agonising over the decision for more than a month, they found themselves standing before the ominous hut, their hearts heavy with apprehension yet clinging to a sliver of hope for a solution.

****

The tantric, sensing the desperation in Sudha and Suresh's demeanour, welcomed them into his humble abode and bid them to take a seat. With a solemn expression, he produced a lemon and deftly wrapped a thread around it, obscuring it from view. He then instructed them to place the wrapped lemon inside a container, fill it with water, and seal it tightly. He instructed them to return on the fifth day with the container.

Despite Suresh's insistence on paying for his guidance, the tantric refused, claiming that his actions were borne out of service rather than monetary gain. With a sense of gratitude and a glimmer of hope, Sudha and Suresh left the hut, clutching the container tightly as they awaited the promised revelation.

On the fifth day, when Sudha cautiously opened the container, she was astounded by what she discovered. The lemon they had placed inside was nowhere to be found; instead, the threads that had bound it were loosely scattered, as if torn apart by unseen forces. Even more unsettling was the sight of the water within the container, which now tinged a deep, ominous red. A shiver ran down Sudha's spine as she exchanged a worried glance with Suresh, realising that the tantrik's ritual had unveiled something inexplicably sinister. With a mixture of apprehension and determination, they knew they had to return to the tantric for answers, their quest for resolution taking on a newfound urgency.

****

As Sudha and Suresh returned to the tantrik's hut, before they could utter a word, the tantric spoke with a knowing look in his eyes. "I know what has transpired," he said solemnly. "The water has turned red as a sign that your house is indeed ensnared in black magic. And the disappearance of the lemon indicates that the malevolent forces at work are of an intense nature."

Sudha and Suresh exchanged a glance, a chill running down their spines at the confirmation of their worst fears. With a sense of urgency and desperation, they turned to the tantric, seeking guidance on how to rid their home of the dark forces that threatened to consume it.

The tantric glanced thoughtfully at some inscriptions written on palm leaves, causing Sudha and Suresh to lean in, eager to understand. However, the language proved incomprehensible to them. Sensing their confusion, the tantric explained that they needed to perform a secret ritual. It would take place in the burial ground under the light of the full moon. They were to dig a hole approximately six feet deep and meditate within it for the entire night. Sudha and Suresh exchanged hesitant glances, the gravity of the ritual weighing heavily upon them.

The tantric, sensing Sudha and Suresh's trepidation, reassured them with a calm demeanour. "I will undertake the ritual on your behalf," he declared firmly. Sudha and Suresh breathed a sigh of relief, grateful for the tantrik's willingness to intervene on their behalf. Trusting in his expertise and guidance, Sudha and Suresh knew that they were in capable hands as they awaited the resolution of their harrowing ordeal.

The tantric pondered for a moment before outlining the materials needed for the ritual: the feathers of an owl, the leaves of the peepal tree, and the sacrifice of a Khadakaknath hen. "It will cost you sixty thousand rupees," he stated matter-of-factly. Suresh's heart sank at the exorbitant cost, knowing it amounted to three months' worth of his hard-earned salary. "Babaji, it's a considerable sum," he confessed, his voice tinged with desperation.

The tantric cast a scrutinising gaze upon Suresh, as though he had made an unrealistic plea.

With a heavy heart and a deep breath, Suresh reluctantly agreed to proceed with the tantrik's proposed ritual, understanding that it was their best chance to put an end to their ordeal once and for all.

The tantric instructed Suresh to return after the full moon night and advised him to stay at a hotel for a few days.

****

After the full moon had passed, Sudha and Suresh visited the tantric once again.

With a serene smile, the tantric explained that the ritual had been successful and they no longer needed to fear the darkness that had plagued their home. Grateful beyond words, Suresh offered the remaining sixty thousand rupees as a token of their appreciation. In the days that followed, the unsettling incidents gradually diminished, and the once ominous fall of lemons on their terrace ceased altogether. Finally, Sudha and Suresh breathed a collective sigh of relief, knowing that the dark chapter of their lives had come to a close.

After three months ......

Life was starting to feel normal again for Sudha. But when she saw Sindhu standing on the road, peeping through the kitchen window, it made her heart sink. Seeing Sindhu brought back scary memories for Sudha. She started feeling really scared again, like before. Sudha and Suresh felt upset because the unsettling things that happened in the past were happening again, ruining their peace. Feeling sad and desperate, Sudha and Suresh knew they had to ask the tantric for help again.

Slowly but surely, as the visits to the tantric continued and the expenses accumulated, Sudha and Suresh found themselves investing a total of 1.5 lakh rupees in their quest for resolution. At first, the problems seemed to subside. However, much to their dismay, the issues would inevitably resurface, casting a shadow over their hopes for a permanent solution. Despite their best efforts and the considerable financial strain, Sudha and Suresh found themselves trapped in a seemingly endless cycle of temporary relief, followed by the return of their haunting troubles.

Following the tantrik's instructions, Sudha and Suresh tried every trick in the book, from temporarily vacating their home for a few days to even installing a white flag on the terrace as a symbol of peace. However, despite their earnest efforts, nothing seemed to work. Frustration and desperation gnawed at Sudha and Suresh as they struggled to break free from the relentless grip of the supernatural, their hopes for a peaceful resolution fading with each failed attempt.

****

"Fear only exists in the mind, and once you confront the unknown, it becomes familiar," Suresh remarked as he and Sudha resolved to strengthen their minds and overcome their fears. Sudha made a conscious effort to ignore Sindhu whenever she appeared, while they both chose to disregard the voodoo dolls on the terrace. Over time, the occurrences gradually faded away.

"You see, Sudha, it was that simple. We just had to ignore it all, and it wouldn't last forever," Suresh reassured her.

However, Sudha remained sceptical. "But Suresh, whenever the tantric performed rituals for us, the occurrences would stop for a while. How is that possible? And what about the vanished lemon?" She questioned.

Suresh pondered her words before suggesting, "Perhaps we should visit the tantric once more and inform him that we are now safe."

The next day, without an appointment, Suresh and Sudha arrived at the tantrik's place. Finding the hut occupied, they decided to wait outside until the current client left.

As Sudha and Suresh waited outside the tantrik's hut, they overheard a woman's voice expressing frustration. "Nothing seems to work; I've spent enough. They are still there," the voice lamented.

The tantric responded reassuringly, "I told you, it takes time. Didn't you see they left the house for some weeks as the ill effects were on them? And they came looking for you, which means the black magic is working."

Sudha, upon hearing this, whispered to Suresh, "Poor client, this sounds like another house issue."

Suresh nodded in agreement, remarking, "Yes, it's not easy to own and stay in a house."

As they continued their discussion, the door suddenly opened, and they were taken aback by the sight that greeted them. The client emerging from the hut locked eyes with them in shock—it was Sindhu.

11. THE MADHU MITAIWALA

As the boy peered through the eyepiece of the bioscope, the operator deftly rotated the wheel. The Taj Mahal emerged first, its majestic silhouette capturing the boy's attention. Then, with a seamless transition, the scene shifted to the delightful sight of Agra's famous Petha, each sugary morsel arranged meticulously on a gleaming plate, tempting the senses with its vibrant colours and sweet fragrance. Accompanying this visual feast was a soft, melodic tune that seemed to dance in harmony with the unfolding spectacle, enveloping the boy in a world of wonder and enchantment.

Next in line was the resplendent Mysore Palace, followed swiftly by the delectable Mysore Pak, the boy's mouth-watering at the sight. The mesmerising show unfolded for a brief 2–3 minutes, showcasing India's iconic landmarks alongside the mouth-watering sweets associated with each place. This was Madhu's ingenious strategy to captivate potential customers.

As the spectacle came to an end, the young boy's attention shifted to the tempting array of sweets neatly displayed on the shelves. Ladoos, jahangiris, barfis, and jalebis—each delicacy seemed to call out to him with its own unique flavour and texture. His eyes sparkled with excitement as he turned to his parents, pleading eagerly to sample half a dozen varieties. His enthusiasm was contagious, filling the air with anticipation and delight as they prepared to indulge in a sweet feast together.

After some gentle persuasion, the parents relented, and the child settled for a couple of sweets. Madhu, the sweet seller, skilfully weighed the chosen treats on an old iron balanced scale, carefully adjusting with half and one kg of iron weights on one side and the sweets on the other. With practiced precision, he wrapped them in newspaper parcels, handing them over to his satisfied customers.

A smile played on Madhu's lips as he completed his first sale of the day, his heart swelling with satisfaction. This was just the beginning of another bustling day at his humble sweet shop, where every treat held a story and every customer left with a taste of India's rich heritage and culinary delights.

****

Madhu's journey to success was anything but smooth. When his father succumbed to old age, Madhu found himself burdened with the weight of responsibility for his family. Left with little more than the knowledge of sweet-making, he embarked on a turbulent path marked by hardship and doubt.

Armed only with determination, Madhu journeyed from town to town and village to village, establishing his modest sweet stall wherever chance allowed. For nearly sixty Jatras spanning the year, he laboured tirelessly, selling his sweets to scrape together a livelihood for himself and his dear ones.

In every town he ventured into, Madhu encountered a unique set of hurdles—ranging from fierce competition to wary customers—but his determination remained steadfast, a beacon guiding him through the storm. Despite scorching summers and biting winters, he stood resolute, his hands tirelessly crafting sweetness amidst life's bitter struggles.

Just as Madhu began to find his footing in the challenging world of sweet-selling, fate dealt him another cruel blow. Stricken with pneumonia, he was forced to take a leave of absence from his business for a gruelling three months. This setback not only dealt a significant blow to his already fragile business but also took a toll on his physical and mental resilience.

The once vibrant and bustling sweet stall now stood silent and empty, a stark reminder of the harsh realities of life. With each passing day of illness, Madhu's ability to cope with stress and maintain the quality of his sweets diminished, casting a shadow of uncertainty over his once-promising venture.

As the days turned into weeks, and the weeks into months, Madhu found himself grappling not only with his failing health but also with the mounting financial burden that weighed heavily on his shoulders. With dwindling sales and the added expenses of raising a growing family, he felt the weight of his responsibilities pressing down upon him like never before.

****

As they say, even the support of a small straw can save a drowning man. For Madhu, that support arrived in the unlikeliest of forms: Naagu. Naagu entered Madhu's life as a coconut picker, arriving at his doorstep with a strength and resilience that left Madhu in awe.

Watching Naagu effortlessly ascend the towering coconut trees and expertly pluck the dried coconuts, Madhu couldn't help but marvel at his stamina and skill.

As Madhu got to know Naagu better, he learned of his background. Naagu hailed from a nearby tribe, descendants of African people brought to the Indian subcontinent by the British centuries ago. Over time, they had integrated with the local Indian population, forming a unique blend of cultures and traditions.

Despite the challenges and prejudices Naagu may have faced as a member of this marginalised community, his spirit remained unbroken.

When Madhu discovered Naagu's previous experience as an assistant to a sweet vendor, a spark of inspiration ignited within him. Recognising Naagu's potential, he promptly hired him as his assistant. Little did Madhu know, this decision would mark the turning point in his fortunes.

Naagu's arrival brought a stroke of luck that Madhu could have never anticipated. It was Naagu who, with his resourcefulness, procured a bioscope from a scrap dealer. Together, they crafted custom-made reels featuring iconic monuments and delectable cuisines, transforming the humble sweet stall into a spectacle that captivated the hearts and imaginations of passers-by.

But it wasn't just the visual spectacle that drew crowds to Madhu's shop. Under Naagu's skilled hands, a new era dawned for Madhu's sweet shop. With his unparalleled expertise, Naagu crafted sweets that surpassed even Madhu's own creations in taste and uniqueness. Despite Madhu's persistent requests for Naagu's recipes, the secret remained closely guarded, adding to the allure of their sweets.

As word of their delectable treats spread like wildfire, lines began to form outside Madhu's shop, each customer eager to sample the unrivalled flavours that only Naagu could conjure. With each passing day, Madhu's income soared to unimaginable heights, thanks to Naagu's culinary wizardry.

****

Amidst the bustling ambiance of their sweet shop, Madhu's attention was drawn to Naagu's agile hands, deftly shaping their signature treats with unmatched finesse. Intrigued by Naagu's exceptional skill, Madhu found himself captivated, pondering over the secret ingredient that seemed to elevate Naagu's creations to unparalleled heights.

Unable to contain his curiosity, Madhu attempted to discreetly observe Naagu as he worked, hoping to catch a glimpse of the elusive recipe. However, Naagu's careful movements thwarted Madhu's attempts, leaving him no closer to uncovering the mystery.

Determined to solve the puzzle, Madhu resorted to more clandestine methods, hiding and peeping around corners in a bid to catch Naagu in the act. Yet, despite his best efforts, the secret remained well-guarded.

All the ingredients for Naagu's culinary masterpieces were familiar to Madhu, save for one elusive element: a mysterious white powder. Naagu added it with a flourish, bestowing upon the sweets a distinct flavour and texture that defied explanation. Despite his persistent efforts to uncover the truth, Madhu was left baffled by the enigmatic ingredient that remained Naagu's closely guarded secret.

After weeks of covert attempts to uncover Naagu's secret ingredient, Madhu decided to confront him directly. With a mixture of apprehension and determination, Madhu approached Naagu, his curiosity getting the better of him.

"Naagu," Madhu began tentatively, "I've been noticing that you add a mysterious white powder to our sweets. Can you tell me what it is?"

Naagu glanced up from his work, his expression unreadable for a moment, before a small smile graced his lips. "Ah, sir," he replied in his calm, steady voice. "That white powder is a closely guarded secret of our tribe. It's simply a blend of herbs passed down through generations."

Madhu's eyebrows furrowed in confusion. "Herbs?" he echoed sceptically.

Naagu nodded. "Yes, herbs with unique properties enhance the flavour and texture of our sweets. It's a tradition among my people, a sacred recipe that we hold."

As suspicions gnawed at Madhu's mind, he couldn't shake the feeling that there was more to Naagu's secret ingredient than mere herbs. Determined to uncover the truth, he confided in his friend Purushottam, and together they hatched a plan to shadow Naagu discreetly.

****

Under the cover of darkness, Madhu and Purushottam trailed Naagu, their hearts pounding with anticipation. Their clandestine pursuit led them to the cremation ground, a place shrouded in solemnity and secrecy. There, amidst the sombre surroundings, they watched in disbelief as Naagu collected leftover bones and began to crush them into a fine powder.

A chill ran down Madhu's spine as he realised the grisly truth behind Naagu's secret ingredient. It wasn't just herbs; it was the ashes of the departed, a macabre addition that lent an eerie depth to Naagu's sweets.

Shocked and horrified by this revelation, Madhu grappled with conflicting emotions. On one hand, he was repulsed by the thought of consuming sweets laced with human remains.

Caught between his conscience and his business aspirations, Madhu faced a moral dilemma unlike any other. Would he continue to turn a blind eye to Naagu's disturbing practices in pursuit of profit, or would he confront Naagu and risk losing everything they had built together?

As the weight of his decision bore down upon him, Madhu knew that the choice he made would irrevocably alter the course of their lives, forever changing the sweet shop that had once been the pride of their community.

As Madhu's frustration reached its breaking point, he decided to confront Naagu head-on, determined to unearth the truth behind the sinister secret of their sweets. With a voice that boomed like thunder, he called out to Naagu, demanding answers with a ferocity that startled even himself.

"Naagu, what the hell are you doing? Is this the secret recipe?" Madhu's words echoed through the air, slicing through the tension that hung between them like a knife.

Naagu, taken aback by the sudden outburst, faltered for a moment before regaining his composure. With an unsettling calmness, he met Madhu's gaze and let out a chilling laugh, sending shivers down his spine.

"Sir, now you know the secret," Naagu admitted, his tone dripping with a macabre certainty. "In our tribe, we believe that by consuming the remains of our departed ancestors, the people of other communities will become closer to us. It's a tradition passed down through generations, a way to forge bonds and bridge the divide between us."

As Naagu's words hung heavy in the air, Madhu felt a knot form in the pit of his stomach. The revelation that their beloved sweets were tainted with such a sinister purpose left him reeling with a mixture of revulsion and disbelief.

As fury surged through Madhu, he clenched his fists around the stick, his knuckles white with rage. With a primal yell, he raised the makeshift weapon, intent on striking Naagu for the betrayal and the sinister truth he had revealed.

But before Madhu could deliver the blow, Naagu's chilling words cut through the air like a dagger. "Sir, you too now have the remains of my ancestors," Naagu declared with a smirk, his tone filled with a haunting finality.

In that moment, a wave of realisation washed over Madhu, the weight of Naagu's words crashing down upon him like a tonne of bricks. As the gravity of the situation sank in, he faltered, the stick slipping from his grasp as he watched Naagu vanish into the dense forest, swallowed by the shadows, never to be seen again.

12. SUSPENDED IN THIN AIR

Ramachandra Master stood in front of the classroom, his words carrying the weight of knowledge and experience. "Gravity," he began, "is the force that pulls objects down to Earth; otherwise, we'd all be suspended in thin air."

As he spoke, a boy named Mahindra raised his hand, his eyes shining with curiosity. Mahindra was from the tribal belt, a first-generation student with a hunger for knowledge that impressed Ramachandra.

Ramachandra nodded, welcoming his question. "Yes, Mahindra?" he prompted, encouraging the young boy's inquiry.

"Is there a way to defy gravity, sir, and remain suspended in thin air?" Mahindra's question hung in the air, sparking a moment of contemplation among his classmates.

Ramachandra smiled at Mahindra's enthusiasm. He believed in encouraging students like Mahindra, who showed a natural aptitude for learning. "For that," he replied, "you would have to travel faster than the escape velocity of 11.2 km/sec from the Earth's surface."

"But sir," Mahindra said again, "what about the birds? They seem to effortlessly glide through the air, defying gravity with every beat of their wings."

A murmur of agreement rippled through the classroom, echoing Mahindra's sentiment.

"Ah, the birds," Ramachandra mused, his eyes alight with enthusiasm. "Indeed, they are masters of the skies, dancing upon the currents of air with grace and precision." He paused, allowing the wonder of nature's marvels to permeate the room.

"However," Ramachandra continued, his tone gentle yet firm, "the birds do not truly defy gravity. Rather, they harness the forces of lift and aerodynamics to overcome its pull." He gestured animatedly, his hands tracing invisible patterns in the air.

"The shape of their wings, the angle of their feathers—every aspect of their anatomy is finely tuned to exploit the principles of flight," Ramachandra explained, his words painting a vivid picture of avian mastery.

Mahindra's eyes widened with understanding. "So, sir," he ventured tentatively, "in a way, the birds are not defying gravity but rather working in harmony with it."

Ramachandra nodded, a proud smile gracing his lips. "Precisely, Mahindra. In the grand symphony of the universe, every creature plays its part, guided by the immutable laws of nature."

Mahindra's brow furrowed deeper, his mind grappling with the boundaries of scientific understanding. "But sir," he persisted, his voice laced with determination, "what if there's a way we haven't discovered yet? Something beyond our current understanding of physics?"

"A valid point, Mahindra," Ramachandra conceded. "Indeed, throughout history, there have been moments when humanity's understanding of the world has been challenged by ground-breaking discoveries and paradigm shifts."

He paced the front of the classroom, his movements deliberate as he pondered the possibilities that lay beyond the confines of conventional wisdom.

"Perhaps," Ramachandra mused, his voice tinged with excitement, "there are phenomena yet to be unearthed, mysteries waiting to be unravelled, that could indeed alter our perception of the laws that govern our universe."

"But until such time," Ramachandra continued, "we must rely on the knowledge and principles that have stood the test of time. It is through diligent observation, rigorous experimentation, and unwavering dedication that we inch ever closer to unlocking the secrets of the cosmos."

Mahindra nodded, a glimmer of understanding dawning in his eyes.

The classroom fell silent, the students lost in contemplation as they pondered the mysteries of flight and the boundless wonders of the world.

****

After the school day ended, the children dispersed to their homes, leaving Ramachandra Master alone in his classroom. With a sigh, he turned to the few books he had on the concept of gravity, hoping to find some insight into Mahindra's persistent question. However, the books offered little beyond the conventional understanding of gravity. Magnetic levitation and sound-based levitation were mentioned, but only in the context of small objects. Taking a few notes to address Mahindra's curiosity in the next class, Ramachandra closed the books and prepared to head home.

As the May holidays had begun, the school was closed, providing him with a break from his teaching duties. He made his way to his home in Sulgod, a small village nestled amidst the rolling hills.

The days passed by slowly, with Ramachandra finding himself restless without the routine of teaching. However, his solitude was interrupted one day by a knock on his door. Opening it, he found Mahindra standing on the other side, a look of excitement on his face.

"Ramachandra sir," Mahindra greeted him eagerly, "I have come to invite you to a special tribal ritual."

Ramachandra raised an eyebrow, intrigued by Mahindra's invitation. "A tribal ritual? What is it about?"

Mahindra explained that the ritual occurred once every 21 years and was attended only by members of his tribe. However, as the son of the tribal chief, Mahindra had been granted permission to invite his teacher. "On a full moon night," Mahindra continued. "The ritual takes place deep in the forest near our tribal settlement. It's a unique experience, and I thought you might find it interesting."

Ramachandra considered the invitation for a moment before nodding in agreement. "Thank you, Mahindra. I would be honoured to join you."

With that, Mahindra and Ramachandra set out on their journey into the heart of the forest.

****

Their journey to the tribal ritual was an adventure in itself. They embarked on the first leg of their trip by bus, traversing through winding roads that cut through the dense forest.

As they disembarked from the bus, Mahindra led the way on foot, guiding Ramachandra through the forest paths.

Mahindra: "We have to walk from here. It's about an eight-hour trek to the tribal village."

Ramachandra: "Eight hours? That's quite a journey."

The trek took them through winding trails and semi-paved roads, surrounded by towering trees and the sounds of wildlife. Along the way, they took breaks to rest and catch their breath.

During one such break, Ramachandra spotted a peculiar creature climbing up a nearby tree. "What's that?" he asked, pointing towards the creature.

Mahindra followed Ramachandra's gaze and let out a soft chuckle. "That's a slow loris," he explained, his voice tinged with a hint of fascination. "We call it the 'wild man.' It's quite fascinating—it's one of the few venomous mammals in the world. Though they have venom, they rarely use it to harm anyone."

Intrigued, Ramachandra observed the creature as it moved gracefully through the branches.

Their journey continued, and they encountered more wildlife along the way. A few spotted deer darted past them, their graceful movements a stark contrast to the rugged terrain.

Ramachandra couldn't help but feel a sense of awe at the sight of these majestic animals in their natural habitat. Concerned about the presence of predators in the forest, he turned to Mahindra for reassurance.

"Do big cats, like leopards, roam around here?" he asked, scanning the dense foliage.

Mahindra nodded. "Yes, sir. Sometimes we spot them, but they rarely pose a threat to humans. They're more afraid of us than we are of them."

Despite his words, Ramachandra couldn't shake off a sense of unease as they pressed on.

As they continued their journey, Mahindra pointed out a massive bird perched on a nearby tree, its wingspan casting a shadow over the forest floor.

"Look, sir, it's a Crested Serpentine Eagle," Mahindra exclaimed, excitement evident in his voice. "It's the biggest bird of prey in this forest."

Ramachandra's eyes widened in surprise as he took in the sight of the majestic bird. The encounter left him speechless, marvelling at the diversity of wildlife that called the forest home.

After hours of trekking through the forest, their journey finally came to an end near a plateau clearing.

As Ramchandra Master and Mahindra arrived at the tribal gathering, they were welcomed with open arms. The tribals greeted them warmly, offering a chair made of coir for Ramchandra to sit on and presenting him with tribal artefacts as gifts. They also offered a meal of fruits and rice grains, a gesture that filled Ramchandra with a sense of pride in his profession.

After some time, a gong rang out, signalling the beginning of the ritual. All the tribals gathered around a small temple at the centre of the clearing, where a strange, half-curved deity known as the "Baital of the Forest" was housed. Ramchandra found himself seated in the front row, a position of honour bestowed upon him by the tribal chief.

The area designated for the ritual was marked by a white powder line, indicating the sacred space that no one could cross. An elderly priest stepped forward to lead the ceremony. Despite his age, he carried himself with strength and dignity, his bare form adorned only by a jockstrap covering his privates. Standing tall at six feet, his bald head and thick metal earring gave him an imposing presence.

With a raised hand, he uttered words that echoed through the surrounding hills, sending a shiver down the spines of even the most seasoned observers.

And so the ritual began, enveloping the village in a haze of ancient mysticism and tradition.

The ritual that unfolded before Ramchandra's eyes was unlike anything he had ever witnessed in the cities. It carried an eerie aura, steeped in ancient traditions and mysticism.

The sight of the tribals lying on the ground with their heads, serving as the platform for the container, was both baffling and intriguing. A container was placed atop their heads, delicately balanced by the trio, and fire sticks were inserted through the gaps between their heads. With careful precision, the sticks were lit, igniting a small fire that began to heat a pot of rice placed on top.

Ramchandra watched in astonishment as the elderly priest meticulously supervised the rice, ensuring it boiled to perfection over the flames. Despite the heat radiating just inches above their heads, the tribals remained still, seemingly unaffected by the intense conditions.

Ramchandra couldn't help but wonder: How did they withstand the heat of the fire without flinching or showing any signs of discomfort? The resilience and endurance displayed by the tribals left him with a newfound appreciation for their ancient rituals and practices.

Next was another amazing ritual.

The air crackled with anticipation as the next ritual unfolded before Ramachandra's eyes, each moment more astonishing than the last.

The old man, with a weathered face marked by years of wisdom, darted around the circle with purpose. With deft hands, he dug a small hole in the earth and gently planted a delicate sapling within it. Turning to the assembled tribals, he issued a challenge—to uproot the plant and cast it away.

Strong and sinewy, the tribals strained against the earth, their muscles bulging with effort as they attempted to dislodge the stubborn roots. Even

Ramachandra, drawn into the fray, lent his strength to the task, but to no avail. The plant held firm, firmly rooted in the soil.

As exhaustion began to set in, a chilling smile crept across the old man's lips. With a casual flick of his wrist, he effortlessly uprooted the plant, casting it aside as if it were a mere twig. The display of strength and control left the onlookers in awe, their murmurs hushed in reverent silence.

But the spectacle was far from over. In a sudden frenzy, the old man seemed to convulse, his body wracked by unseen forces. The tribe erupted into a chorus of eerie chants, their voices rising and falling in a haunting cadence. It was the unmistakable sign that Baital had entered the old man's body, invoking powers beyond mortal comprehension.

Under the pale moonlight, the old man, now possessed by the primal spirit, danced with abandon. His movements were untamed, wild, and erratic, as he leapt into the circle with primal ferocity.

In a macabre turn of events, a group of tribals ascended a makeshift platform, bearing baskets filled with unsuspecting hens. They hurled the hens, one after another, into the circle. With swift and savage motions, the possessed man, now known as Bimba, seized the birds one by one, his jaws closing around their necks with a sickening snap.

The air was filled with the shrill cries of the dying birds, mingling with the primal roar of the possessed man. Feathers flew and blood spattered as Bimba dispatched the hapless creatures with ruthless efficiency. Ramchandra recoiled in horror at the barbarity unfolding before him, his heart heavy with sorrow.

As the last of the hens fell silent, their lifeblood staining the earth, Bimba cast their lifeless bodies from the circle with a callous disregard. The tribals gathered the fallen birds, their faces alight with anticipation for the feast that awaited them, leaving Ramachandra to grapple with the dark spectacle he had witnessed.

Ramachandra thought he had seen enough, but the final ritual was far from over. This concluding ceremony packed the most suspense, unfolding with an otherworldly energy that left Ramchandra both bewildered and mesmerised.

The tribals orchestrated a symphony of light and sound, setting the stage for a spectacle unlike any Ramchandra had witnessed before. Mashaal's flames, flickering in the night air, were positioned around the circle, casting an ethereal glow upon the gathered throng. Kerosene-lit torches illuminated the scene, their fiery tendrils dancing in the darkness.

In the heart of the circle, bamboo-made instruments formed a triangular formation, their rhythmic drumming reverberating through the forest with an intensity that seemed to shake the very earth. Special drums crafted from monitor lizard skin emitted a primal beat, each strike echoing across the landscape like a thunderous proclamation.

As the drumming reached a crescendo, the tribal men and women joined in a haunting chorus, their voices blending with the pulsating rhythm of the drums. The chant, "bhooba bhooba bhooba ta tum bhooba," filled the air with an eerie resonance, casting a spell of anticipation over the assembled gathering.

Then, in a moment that defied rational explanation, Ramachandra felt a jolt of disbelief ripple through his consciousness. His gaze fixed upon Bimba, who stood at the centre of the circle, his form bathed in the surreal glow of the ritual. Without warning, Bimba began to ascend into the air, his body rising effortlessly above the ground.

For three mesmerizing minutes, Bimba hovered in mid-air, a testament to the mysterious forces at play within the confines of the ritual circle. As he descended to the earth, his body trembling with the remnants of unearthly power, Ramchandra's mind raced with questions, grappling with the enigma of what he had witnessed.

As night fell and the feast began, Ramachandra found himself unable to shake the lingering sense of wonder and bewilderment. When offered a meal of chicken, he politely declined, his mind still reeling from the inexplicable events of the ritual.

During the feast, Ramchandra seized the opportunity to inquire about the tribe's ancient traditions, particularly the phenomenon of Bimba's levitation. The chief, steeped in the wisdom of generations past, offered an explanation rooted in the mysticism of the land.

"This tradition has been followed for centuries," the chief explained. "Once every 21 years, we perform this ritual, and it is only possible in this sacred place. The secret lies in the precise rhythm of drums and chants, which echo across the hills and invoke the spirits of the land. These hills respond back to us in the echo's, and the person in that circle levitates."

Ramachandra's mind raced with questions as he pondered the enigma before him. Was it sound-based levitation, as the chief suggested? Perhaps a lost science, hidden within the depths of time? Whatever the answer, the ritual had left an indelible mark upon Ramachandra's soul, igniting a thirst for knowledge that would endure long after the echoes of the drums had faded into the night.